ns™

# THE NEED TO KNOW LIBRARY

# EVERYTHING YOU NEED TO KNOW ABOUT
# GUN VIOLENCE

ADAM FURGANG

Jefferson Madison
Regional Library
Charlottesville, Virginia

Published in 2018 by The Rosen Publishing Group, Inc.
29 East 21st Street, New York, NY 10010

Copyright © 2018 by The Rosen Publishing Group, Inc.

First Edition

All rights reserved. No part of this book may be reproduced in any form without permission in writing from the publisher, except by a reviewer.

**Library of Congress Cataloging-in-Publication Data**

Names: Furgang, Adam, author.
Title: Everything you need to know about gun violence / Adam Furgang.
Description: New York : Rosen Publishing, 2018. | Series: The need to know library | Audience: Grades 7-12. | Includes bibliographical references and index.
Identifiers: LCCN 2017002120 | ISBN 9781508174042 (library-bound) | ISBN 9781508174028 (pbk.) | ISBN 9781508174035 (6-pack)
Subjects: LCSH: Gun control—United States—Juvenile literature. | Firearms ownership—United States—Juvenile literature. | Violent crimes—United States—Juvenile literature.
Classification: LCC HV7436 .F87 2018 | DDC 363.330973—dc23
LC record available at https://lccn.loc.gov/2017002120

*Manufactured in China*

# CONTENTS

**INTRODUCTION** ................................................................. 4

**CHAPTER ONE**
**THE SECOND AMENDMENT AND GUN HISTORY** ................... 7

**CHAPTER TWO**
**GUN VIOLENCE TODAY** ........................................................18

**CHAPTER THREE**
**HOW DOES THE UNITED STATES COMPARE**
**TO OTHER COUNTRIES?** .......................................................27

**CHAPTER FOUR**
**EXPLORING THE ISSUES** .......................................................34

**CHAPTER FIVE**
**WHAT CAN I DO ABOUT GUN VIOLENCE?** ............................42

**GLOSSARY** ..............................................................................54
**FOR MORE INFORMATION** .....................................................56
**FOR FURTHER READING** ........................................................58
**BIBLIOGRAPHY** ......................................................................59
**INDEX** ....................................................................................62

# INTRODUCTION

If you watch the news, it might seem like there is new evidence of gun violence every day. It might also seem like the problem is worsening. But if you look at statistics gathered by the Centers for Disease Control and Prevention, gun violence overall in the United States has been dropping steadily since the 1990s. In 1993, firearms killed 7 out of every 100,000 Americans. But by 2013, that number changed to only about 3.6 out of every 100,000 Americans. Nonfatal crimes with firearms also declined during the same time period.

There are a couple of reasons why we hear about gun violence so much on the news. One is that more Americans are paying attention to gun violence. In fact, the issue has become one that polarizes, or divides, people. Some want more laws to restrict the use of guns, in hopes of cutting down on violence and death. Others feel that restricting people's access to guns would go against the Constitution of the United States.

Another reason for the proliferation of incidences of gun violence in the news is simply that it is a problem that still eludes a solution. In 2014 alone, according to CNN, more than 30,000 Americans died from gun violence. The phenomenon of mass shootings, attacks on four or more people, in particular, have created anxiety

# INTRODUCTION    5

President Barack Obama discusses the epidemic of gun violence in America with CNN's Anderson Cooper.

that a large number of people at a time can become vulnerable to gun violence. In 2015, there were 294 mass shootings in the United States in 274 days. The effects of mass shootings are vast and troublesome no matter where they occur.

In addition to mass shootings, gun violence can manifest itself in other ways. Gangs in urban, rural, and suburban areas rely on guns and may use them against rivals. Robberies often involve guns. Individual disputes, from property disputes to domestic issues, sometimes end with the use of guns. Suicide is another tragic example of the use of guns. Although guns are not the most common method for suicide attempts, they are the most successful. According to *Harvard Public Health* magazine, 85 percent of people who attempt suicide with a gun end up dying. That compares starkly to other methods, such as attempted drug overdoses, which are just 3 percent lethal. The damage of a gun is massive and irreversible.

It's important for young people to understand the effects of gun violence on our culture. Even though there are different sides to this controversial issue, it's important for people on both sides of the issue to understand as much as possible about it. It's only then that young people can make informed decisions about what the future of gun violence and gun control will look like. Guns in the United States have followed a certain trajectory in history, spotted with laws that follow (or failed to manifest) on the heels of gun violence in America, and movements that passionately fight for or against what guns do and represent. But the American model of gun legislation isn't the only example, so it is useful to compare gun control in the US to that in other countries. One last important point to discuss is how young people can engage in a knowing way with the possibilities of influencing legislation or encountering handling guns or delicate situations with great potential to end badly.

CHAPTER ONE

# THE SECOND AMENDMENT AND GUN HISTORY

When Americans think about the future of gun control and how gun violence will affect the nation, it is important to think about the history of guns as well. The story of how guns have shaped our nation and its laws are a great limit to how much change is possible in the direction of restricting or enabling gun users.

## THE BEGINNING OF THE RIGHT TO BEAR ARMS

When the Constitution was written, the Founding Fathers hoped to set down a list of basic rights and laws for all American citizens. The original document, signed in 1787, focused much on the basic rights of life, liberty, and the pursuit of happiness. The writers purposely left room for the document to be changed, through the passing of amendments, or additions. The first ten amendments are called the Bill of Rights. They named specific rights that Americans are entitled to and that state and local laws should respect when they write their own laws.

The Second Amendment involves gun control and the right to own and carry firearms. Congress passed the Second Amendment on September 25, 1789, and it was ratified, or made legal and official, on December 15, 1791. The amendment states, "A well regulated Militia, being necessary to the security of a free State, the right of the people to keep and bear Arms, shall not be infringed."

The wording of the amendment hints at the history of the country and how it was formed. A militia is a military presence that comes from the civilian population. It is often used to help a regular army when needed, such as in the case of an emergency or attack. In some cases, a militia may be all that is available to fight against oppressors such as other armies and governments. The founders thought that if citizens were kept from being able to form a militia, the country's freedom could be at risk. Militias often supply their own weapons, so the right of an average citizen to keep firearms was very important.

As the nation grew and changed, the right to bear arms became important for frontiersmen and farmers. The right to bear arms allowed them to protect themselves, their families, and their property from the attack of hostile Native Americans or outlaws. It helped them to hunt and feed their families, and to infiltrate land in the west that they hadn't yet taken over and annexed.

Today, the country does not have the same concerns as in the past. A strong army and National Guard make a militia unnecessary. And, it is the job of police to protect citizens and property. In addition, technology has made

# THE SECOND AMENDMENT AND GUN HISTORY

This hand-colored woodcut depicts British soldiers attacking the Patriots during the Battle of Bunker Hill.

guns deadlier and faster than ever. To some people, the current abilities of some guns seem too powerful to authorize just anyone to access. Yet, our rights are guaranteed.

Modern weapons have become a political issue because in order to change the way guns are bought and sold, new laws need to be put into place. This results in a divide between people who want stricter gun control laws and those who feel that restricting gun rights is a violation of the Second Amendment. Traditionally, Democrats want to see stricter gun control laws. Republicans want to prioritize Second Amendment rights.

## GUNS OF THE PAST

At the time that the Bill of Rights was written, guns were a very different weapon. People carried muskets, which were difficult to conceal and could take over a minute to reload. The user had to load gunpowder and reload ammunition into a long chamber, being careful not to make the gunpowder ignite and explode. The musket was aimed over the user's shoulder, and it was accurate up to about 80 yards (73 meters). Muskets were used for military purposes or for hunting.

There were many weapons of choice in the 1700s. The pistols available for carrying around and for self-defense were much weaker and less accurate than the ones used today. A popular weapon, called a flintlock pocket pistol, came in various sizes and

A musket (*pictured*) was the gun that was commonly used in the 1700s. It took a long time to load and was difficult to handle, compared to today's firearms.

was often carried in a holster. These guns were popular until the late 1700s when they were replaced with more powerful and accurate guns. Muskets and pistols both evolved during the 1700s, though they were usually slow to reload. By the start of the Civil War, gun technologies developed to allow for cartridges that could fire up to seven shots in fifteen seconds. It eventually became an important tool for Civil War soldiers. During this same time period, the Gatling gun became the most advanced and powerful gun, able to fire 200 rounds per minute. It is considered an ancestor to the modern machine gun. The spring-loaded and hand-cranked gun became a standard weapon for the US Army until it was replaced by single-barrel machine guns with even more rapid-fire power.

## GUNS TODAY

Today, people still use rifles and pistols, just as in the 1700s, but the technology is so much more advanced that the weapons have become more powerful than ever. Some guns on the market have features that make the guns quieter, easier to aim, or easier and faster to reload. Removable sections, called clips, can make loading and unloading ammunition very quick and easy.

Some fire rapidly and repeatedly for long periods of time before needing to be reloaded. These are called automatic weapons. A machine gun is a type of automatic weapon that can shoot bullets continuously as the shooter keeps a finger down on the trigger. While this type of gun is legal, there are many restrictions for owning and using it.

Semiautomatic weapons are also fast and can easily shoot a large number of rounds. They are less restricted than automatic weapons. One of the most popular semiautomatic weapons is called the AR-15. The "AR" stands for ArmaLite, the company that developed the gun in the 1950s. It fires only one round of ammunition with each pull of the trigger. The gun looks like a military rifle and was originally designed for use in war, but it is adapted for civilian use. These guns are used for sporting purposes and also for illegal activities.

## WHAT CAN AN AR-15 DO TO THE BODY?

With advances in technology comes a huge jump in the effectiveness of guns. After the slow-loading guns of the past, semiautomatic and automatic weapons were developed to inflict a lot of damage on the body. According to *Wired* magazine, a trauma surgeon from the University of Arizona has operated on patients who have been shot with different types of guns. He states that the damage a handgun does is a lot less than what an AR-15 does because the speed of a bullet coming out of a handgun is a lot less than that of an AR-15. At times, the handgun bullet can be stopped by bone or pass through a section of the body, cutting more like a knife. The AR-15 bullet works at a much higher speed, causing

# THE SECOND AMENDMENT AND GUN HISTORY | 13

**ripples in tissue as it passes through and damaging a larger area of the body. The force of the bullets can shatter bone, burst arteries, and do damage that surgery can do little to repair.**

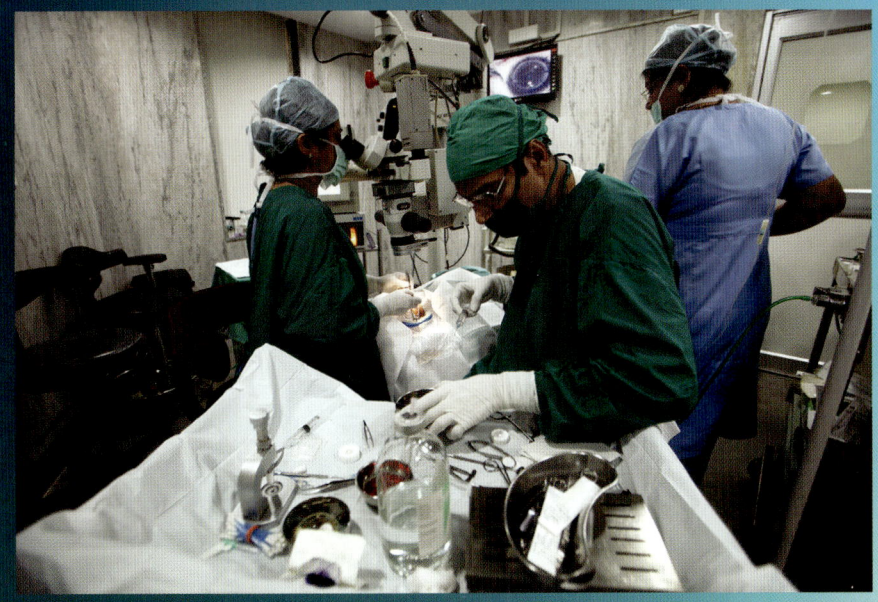

Surgeons must use modern technology to help people recover from the damage that today's firearms can cause to the human body.

According to *PBS NewsHour*, the AR-15 is one of the most common guns of choice for recent mass shootings. The reasons may be because it is relatively easy to obtain and it can inflict a lot of damage in a very short amount of time. Or maybe it is a common choice because of its popularity.

While the Second Amendment is an important part of the American Constitution, the problems inflicted by modern weapons such as the AR-15 make it clear why some people think more control is needed for the types of weapons that should be able to get into the hands of ordinary citizens. Many people who want stricter gun control would like to see a ban on many semiautomatic weapons, including the AR-15.

## ACCORDING TO THE LAW

In the United States, there have been gun control laws for many years. The Gun Control Act of 1968 makes it illegal to sell firearms to anyone under the age of eighteen or to anyone who has a criminal record, mental disability, or dishonorable military discharge. The law also prohibits sales to illegal aliens. Since the Brady Handgun Violence Prevention Act of 1993 was passed, federal law requires a background check to be completed that may allow denial of the sale within three days. This process is required for all people who don't have a license to purchase a firearm. None of these restrictions are foolproof in preventing gun violence, and many critics claim that gun control does not help in reducing crime or gun violence. Further, a study in the *Harvard Journal of Law & Public Policy* state, "It may be speculated that murder rates around the world would be higher if guns were more available. But there is simply no evidence to support this." The study found that Russia has very strict gun control laws, but it still has

## THE NATIONAL RIFLE ASSOCIATION

One of the most influential organizations in America regarding gun control and gun laws is the National Rifle Association (NRA). The organization started in 1871 to help people increase their rifle skills. It expanded over the years, getting involved in training programs for law enforcement and offering courses and information about the safe and responsible use of guns. Today, it continues to do those things and also works to protect the Second Amendment. According to its website, it is one of the most vocal voices for not restricting the rights of citizens to bear arms in any way. In order to do this and influence laws, NRA members get involved in writing to Congress to express their opinions and voting for candidates who do not want restrictions on the Second Amendment, even through state or local law changes.

a high murder rate. The murder rate in Russia is four times as high as it is in the United States, but there are a lot fewer guns. This statistic suggests that eliminating guns does not eliminate murder or violence.

While guns are allowed in every state, states may place restrictions on where and how the guns can be used, purchased, or carried. For example, a state law in Florida restricts the purchase of a gun for those without permits with a holding period of three days so that authorities can search the criminal record of the person buying the gun. A permit is also necessary to conceal a weapon or bring it to public places in a hidden capacity.

Gun dealers like this one must be aware of the laws governing gun sales. Interstate compliance for particularly spread-out dealers is even more difficult because laws vary from state to state.

Local gun restrictions may differ widely from big cities to rural areas. In rural communities, guns are used for hunting and are more commonly used. There are often fewer restrictions on guns in rural communities.

And then there are laws on conduct regarding gun usage. "Stand Your Ground" laws are laws that ensure the rights of citizens to use guns in the case of self-defense. The first state to adopt such a law was Florida, which did so in 2005. The law allowed a person to protect himself as a last resort to avoid death or great bodily harm. It also allowed people to protect their home and property from intruders meaning harm.

Twenty-two additional states passed similar legislation allowing people to "stand their ground" with firearms as a last-resort deadly force to protect themselves.

The strength of the law was put to the test in 2012 when seventeen-year old Trayvon Martin was shot and killed by twenty-eight-year old George Zimmerman in Florida. Martin was an unarmed African American teen that Zimmerman followed around the neighborhood of Martin's father's fiancée. Zimmerman used the Stand Your Ground argument in his trial. The jury acquitted Zimmerman of second degree murder and manslaughter in 2013.

CHAPTER TWO

# GUN VIOLENCE TODAY

The idea that guns get into the hands of criminals is one of the biggest concerns of all lawmakers and citizens. The desire to protect the Second Amendment sometimes seems at odds with the desire to control crime and promote public health. No matter which side of the debate a person is on, both sides agree that the effects of gun violence today are far-reaching.

## GUN VIOLENCE BREAKDOWN

There are several ways that gun violence can enter into one's life. One way is inner city or suburban or rural gang violence. Any robbery that happens might involve a gun. Individual and private arguments might include domestic disputes or professional rivalries that get out of control. Suicides and accidental gun violence are also big concerns.

# GUN VIOLENCE TODAY 19

Boston Police Department deputy superintendent William Gross discusses guns that his office confiscated in 2012.

## THE COLLECTIVE VIOLENCE OF GANGS

Gangs sometimes deal in guns that are illegal, such as automatic weapons, and they sometimes use guns that are legal to obtain. Selling either of these types of guns results in their illicit use during several activities: drug deals that go badly, drive-bys, and gang warfare. And while gangs may be interested in using their guns only on enemies, anyone caught in the crossfire is liable to become a victim.

For a more holistic understanding of the landscape of gangs throughout the United States, consider this: according to a report for ABC News compiled by the Federal Bureau of Investigation (FBI), Chicago Police Department, and National Gang Intelligence Center, gang activity nationwide increased 40 percent between 2009 and 2011. For a city like Chicago, Illinois, black males between ages seventeen and twenty-five with a criminal record are as likely to be murder victims as they are to be the ones accused of murder.

While Chicago in particular has one of the worst gang problems in the United States, gangs aren't limited to the stereotypical poor, urban neighborhood with a high concentration of minority populations, failing schools, and a weak economy. Many poor rural areas have the same circumstances concerning the proliferation of crime as poor urban areas because of the common factor of *poverty*, not race. That poverty often produces similar rates of crime in rural areas as urban areas when it comes to possession of drugs and weapons.

## VIOLENCE OUTSIDE OF GANGS

There are many instances in which people choose to commit violence for their own personal gain or satisfaction, and they sometimes use guns to do so. According to the National Institute of Justice, data collected by the FBI in 2011 showed that "firearms were used in 68 percent of murders, 41 percent of robbery offenses and 21 percent of aggravated assaults nationwide." The study also showed that most homicides in the United States were committed with handguns.

Suicide is another type of violence that has nothing to do with gangs. According to the Centers for Disease Control (CDC), the number of suicides in America has increased by 24 percent in the last fifteen years. Occurrences of suicides by guns has also increased. Because it is the most successful form of attempted suicide, removing guns as a means to end one's life has become an increasing concern for gun control advocates.

Another type of gun violence is accidents. According to WISQARS Injury Mortality Reports, there were 606 deaths in 2010 that were a result of accidental firearm injuries. Children under the age of six accounted for the firing in about 8 percent of those accidental shootings. Gun control advocates have used statistics like these to help strengthen their arguments for childproof safety locks on guns and mandatory loading indicators to let the user know that a gun is loaded.

## MASS SHOOTINGS

Even though the United States makes up just 5 percent of the world's population, research by the FBI indicates that the US has had 31 percent of the world's mass shootings between 1966 and 2012. These shootings occur for different reasons, ranging from anger toward being bullied (Columbine High School), mental illness (Sandy Hook Elementary School), anger toward the political climate in the United States (Pulse nightclub), a

## QUESTIONING SELF-DEFENSE

Law enforcement officers deal with real threats to their safety on a regular basis. But there have been many incidences in which black men have been executed by police officers under the guise of self-defense. One example is South Carolina resident Walter Scott. Scott was shot to death by Michael Slager, who was a police officer at the time, during a traffic stop. The shooting was caught on video, and it clearly showed Slager shooting Scott in the back as Scott was fleeing. The video then shows Slager placing his taser next to Scott's body to frame him.

The Black Lives Matter movement works to fight the violence and systemic racism that is commonly directed toward black people in the United States.

general lack of attention to the emotional state of culprits, easy access to guns, a blatant lack of respect for life, a desire to destroy as much as possible in a short period of time, and several other factors.

No matter what side someone is on about gun control, the response to mass shootings is immediate sorrow and sadness. In fact, the many speeches President Barack Obama gave after the many mass shootings that occurred during his presidency to help address the nation's shock and sadness earned him the nickname "Consoler-in-Chief," which was a play on the president's title of "Commander-in-Chief."

## COLUMBINE HIGH SCHOOL

On April 20, 1999, at Columbine High School in Littleton, Colorado, students Eric Harris and Dylan Klebold each brought several assault rifles, shotguns, and hand grenades to school, hidden under long trenchcoats. The teens entered the school cafeteria and began a shooting spree. In the end, thirteen students were killed and more than twenty others were injured. The boys then killed themselves in the school.

The incident shocked the nation and sparked a debate about gun control, since the boys obtained their guns illegally and some of the guns had once been on a list of banned guns. The debate about guns that was reinvigorated by Columbine (and inspired by incidents of gun violence in the 60s and 1981) continues today.

## SANDY HOOK ELEMENTARY SCHOOL

On December 14, 2012, twenty-year-old Adam Lanza entered Sandy Hook Elementary School in Newtown, Connecticut, with an AR-15 rifle and several pistols. He killed six adults and twenty students between the ages of six and seven. Like the shooters at Columbine, Lanza also took his own life when his shooting spree was finished. Lanza's mother legally acquired the guns that Lanza used during the massacre. Lanza used the weapons to kill her first before taking them on his murder spree at his former elementary school. The young age of the victims of this mass shooting were particularly difficult for Americans to grasp.

## PULSE NIGHTCLUB

Although it seems that many mass shootings occur at school, there are other places where mass shooters do their work. They have committed murders at community gatherings of politicians, at malls, in movie theaters, and even at nightclubs. On June 12, 2016, Omar Mateen entered the Pulse nightclub in Orlando, Florida, and opened fire on the crowd, killing forty-nine people and injuring fifty-three others. Semiautomatic weapons were used in the attack, allowing for the maximum amount of damage in a short amount of time. The guns he used were legally purchased, and during the attack

The Pulse nightclub (*pictured*) in Orlando, Florida, is decorated with tributes to the forty-nine victims of the June 2016 mass shooting.

Mateen declared allegiance to the leader of the Islamic State. This raised questions among the public about the process used to allow people to purchase guns.

Each mass shooting presents unique circumstances regarding how the guns were obtained and whether any changes to laws would have prevented that slaughter from happening in the first place. And with each new mass shooting, the controversial issue of gun control is brought to the nation's attention again.

# MYTHS AND FACTS

**MYTH:** Most people who carry guns are criminals.

**FACT:** While criminals may obtain access to guns, there is no correlation between gun ownership and criminal record. According to the *Journal of Criminal Justice*, studies that show a link between gun ownership and crime are flawed. An average citizen who owns a gun is not more likely to be a criminal than someone who does not own a gun.

**MYTH:** Most people who commit mass shootings obtain their guns illegally.

**FACT:** According to NBC News, more than 80 percent of guns used in mass shootings were obtained legally by the shooter. While one shooter may have obtained some of the guns used legally and others illegally, statistics do not break down the figures in such detail. Some believe that this means that the systems in place for checking the background of a gun buyer are not working.

**MYTH:** Changing gun laws will lower the instances of gun deaths and gun violence.

**FACT:** While changing laws may make it harder to get guns into the hands of criminals legally, criminals may still be able to obtain guns illegally. Someone willing to commit a crime with a gun may be just as likely to commit a crime to obtain the gun.

CHAPTER THREE

# HOW DOES THE UNITED STATES COMPARE TO OTHER COUNTRIES?

Do many countries have mass shootings and gun violence statistics similar to those of the United States? What about gun-free violence and murder? The fact is that there's a big difference between the statistics in the United States and elsewhere around the world.

## WORLDWIDE DEATH RATES

According to CBS News, Americans are ten times more likely to be killed by guns than people in other developed countries around the world. Gun-related murders in the United States are also twenty-five times higher than in other developed nations. Gun-related suicides are eight times higher than in other developed countries. In terms of accidental deaths, Americans are six times more likely to be killed by a gun accidentally than people from other nations. The statistics reported by the news agency were obtained through a 2016 study conducted by the *American Journal of Medicine*.

**28** | EVERYTHING YOU NEED TO KNOW ABOUT GUN VIOLENCE

The dangers of improperly storing a gun are threefold: someone might use it by accident, a child may gain access to it, or someone who means the gun owner harm can more easily access the weapon.

With statistics like these, people advocating for gun control may say that firearms are killing us rather than protecting us. But comparing the American murder rate of guns to countries that restrict guns much more vigorously is somewhat disparate because those who want to commit violence and don't have access to guns would simply rely on different means. For a more equivalent comparison, overall, the American murder rate is 3.9 per 100,000. That's significantly lower than the world average, 6.2 per 100,000, but higher than most European and Asian countries.

And there's more to what guns are doing than just committing crimes as a means of causing death. In other words, killing someone isn't always a denouncable act that should be described as murder. According to the National Safety Council, guns are used more than eighty times more often to protect people's lives in self-defense than for any other reason. According to *Newsweek* magazine, citizens with guns kill more criminals than police do, and only 2 percent of civilian shootings involve cases of mistaken identity in identifying the criminal. These statistics indicate that guns are working the way they may have been intended to work. Nonetheless, it seems that countries with smaller murder rates that restrict guns much more thoroughly must have something in place of guns that is sufficient protection for the people who live there.

For a different perspective, it may help to consider how other countries around the world handle gun control and gun ownership.

Combat units in the Israeli army (*pictured*) consist of citizens. They will go through military training that includes the proper handling and use of firearms.

## GUN LAWS AROUND THE WORLD

According to *PBS NewsHour*, different countries have vastly different laws about gun control. In Canada, federal laws require all gun owners to be at least eighteen years old and have a gun license that includes a background check and a course in public safety. Anyone who wishes to have a handgun, semiautomatic or automatic weapon must get a federal registration certificate. Compared to the United States, where there are about

# HOW DOES THE UNITED STATES COMPARE TO OTHER COUNTRIES? | 31

## FIREARMS IN JAPAN

According to the *Washington Post*, there are many restrictions for owning a gun in Japan. First, you must attend a class about gun laws and safety, and then pass a written test about what you learned. Paperwork must also be submitted to provide details about your family, education, and other personal and health issues. A full-day training course is also required, to makes sure you know the basics of loading and shooting a gun. The

Japan requires firearms to be stored in a locker like this so that they are not easy for just anyone to access.

(*continued on the next page*)

> (*continued from the previous page*)
>
> **police visit your home to make sure you have the proper place to store the gun if and when you pass the training course. Applying for a permit allows you to begin the process of purchasing a gun, which must be inspected at a local police station and registered. Storing the gun also involves many restrictions. The law requires a gun locker with three locks on the outside and a metal chain around the trigger guard when it is being stored. A separate location is required for the ammunition to be stored in. Authorities regularly monitor the storage of the firearms in people's homes. These restrictions are able to be enforced due to the small number of gun owners in the country.**

eighty-nine firearms per 100 people, Canada has about thirty-one firearms for every 100 people.

In Israel, most citizens are part of the armed forces for several years and receive weapons training when they get out of high school. Even in a society so trained in how to use guns, there are severe restrictions for ownership. A citizen or permanent resident interested in buying a gun must be at least twenty-one years old and explain the reason for owning the weapon, such as self-defense or hunting. Israel has about seven firearms per 100 people.

In the United Kingdom, mass shootings prompted the restriction of guns. In 1987, in Hungerford, England, a gunman named Michael Robert Ryan used semiautomatic rifles and a handgun to kill sixteen people and then himself. The six-hour long incident west of London prompted the introduction of the Firearms Act, which was an amendment to the nation's already strict gun control. The amendment added many new weapons to the banned list and added increased requirements for owning firearms. Scotland had a mass shooting in 1996 with a similar result, and the government put a temporary gun buyback program in place to help take tens of thousands of guns out of circulation in the country. The United Kingdom has about six firearms per 100 people.

Gun ownership laws in Japan are considered to be the most restrictive in the world. It is illegal to own a gun in Japan, with very few exceptions. The nation has the lowest gun-homicide rate in the world. Only one in ten million people are killed each year due to gun violence. Some people believe the nation's low crime rate makes it possible for the country to have such restrictions because people see no need for weapons. Japan has less than one firearm per 100 people.

CHAPTER FOUR

# EXPLORING THE ISSUES

The gun control debate is not just one single debate. There are fifty states, and each has its own regulations regarding selling, acquiring, storing, and using guns. Gun control legislation goes down even to the local level, where change can be made and healthy debates can be had among citizens to affect change.

## DO GUN LAWS MAKE A DIFFERENCE?

Pro-gun advocates think that the presence of laws are insufficient protection to the dangers guns can pose, whereas gun control advocates are more interested in alternative means of protection.

According to the Law Center, California has the toughest gun laws in the nation for all types of firearms. Purchasers need licenses to own or purchase a gun, and there are waiting periods before they may receive them. There are universal background checks for all firearms and bans on carrying most types of weapons in public. Northeastern states such as New York, New

# EXPLORING THE ISSUES

**License To Carry Concealed Pistol, Revolver, or Other Firearm Within the State of California**

Issued By:

Agency: Culver City P.D.  Date of Issue: 01/26/01
"ORI": CA0191800  Expiration Date: 01/26/03
Local Agency Number: N6649  CII #: 09923456

☐ Initial
☒ Subsequent

TED COOKE, Chief of Police
Signature and Title of Issuing Officer

## SECTION A

Name of Licensee: Robert BLAKE
Residence Address: ▬▬▬▬▬▬▬▬
City: Culver City  Zip: 90232  County: Los Angeles
Business Address: Same  Occupation: Actor
Birthdate: 9/18/33  Hgt: 5-6  Wgt: 155  Eye Color: Blu  Hair Color: Brn
LICENSE TYPE: Employ. ☐  Standard ☒  Judicial ☐  Reserve ☐  Custodial ☐

## SECTION B - Description of Weapon(s)

| Manufacturer | Serial Number | Caliber | Model |
|---|---|---|---|
| S&W | BKR8297 | .38 | .38 |
| Glock | SK402 | .40 | 23 |
| S&W | J385440 | .38 | Airweight |

Restrictions (if any): ▬▬▬▬▬▬▬▬

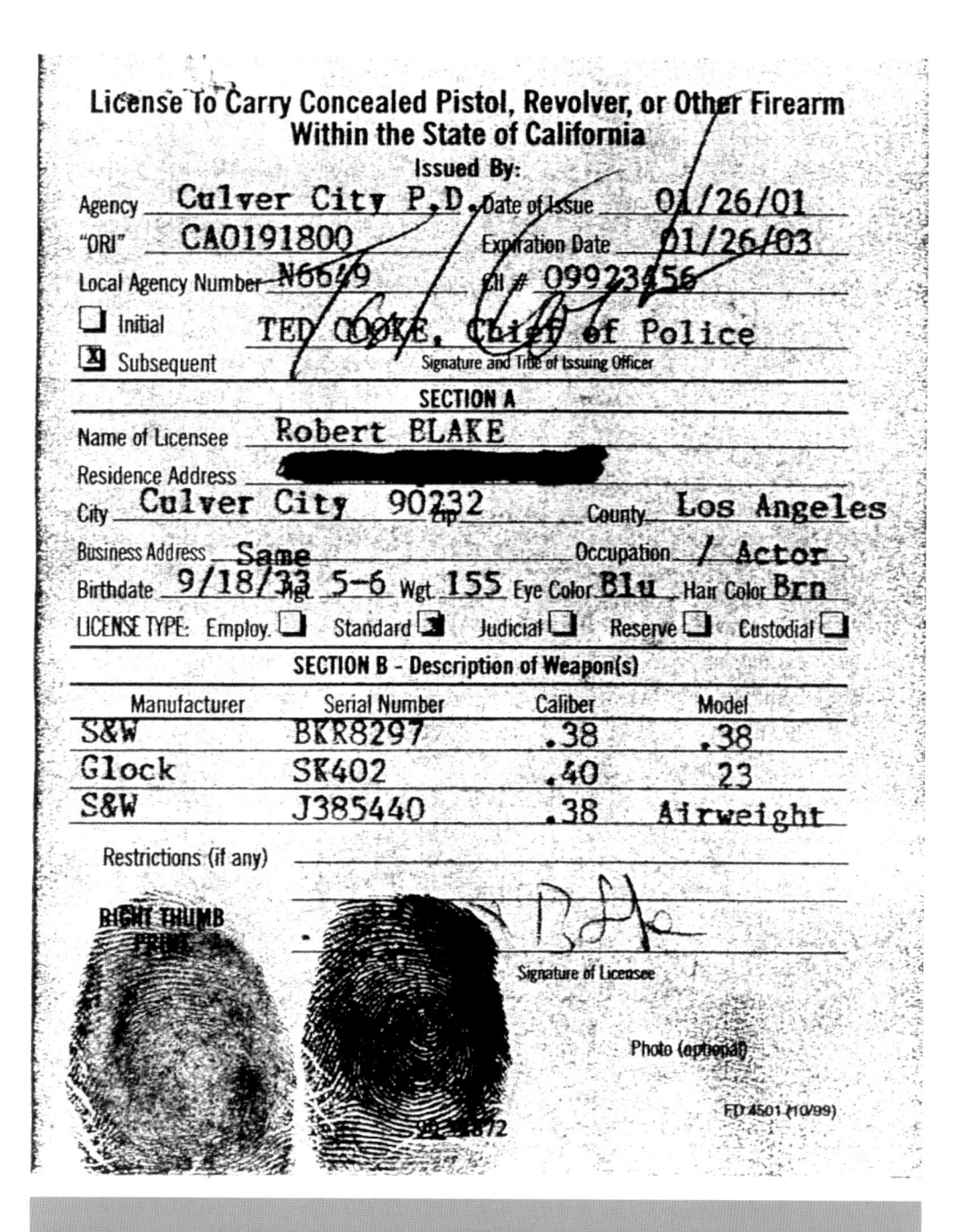

RIGHT THUMB

Signature of Licensee

Photo (optional)

FD 4501 (10/99)

California requires gun owners in that state to have a license (*pictured*) for all types of firearms.

Jersey, Massachusetts, Connecticut, and Rhode Island have similarly strict laws about weapons, including a ban on assault weapons, or semiautomatic or automatic firearms with detachable ammunition magazines, a pistol grip, and other features that vary by jurisdiction.

Despite California's strict laws, they still have incidences of gun violence and mass shootings. In December 2015, a mass shooting took place in San Bernardino, California, in which Syed Farook and his wife, Tashfeen Malik, killed fourteen people and seriously injured twenty-two others at Farook's workplace. According to the *New York Times*, the guns used in the incident were obtained legally.

In the case of the San Bernardino shooters, gun rights supporters would argue that no laws could have prevented the attack. For starters, if a person is willing to commit a crime and murder innocent people, they are likely willing to break the law to obtain a gun to do so. The gun market reacts to bans by offering alternatives, and buying firearms online is not difficult, even for someone from a state with strict laws. Further, avoiding banned brands or features may be easy for someone intent on legally buying a gun. Additionally, if law enforcement was unwilling to monitor Farook's activity after noticing his contact with individuals who were suspected of terroristic allegiance before the attack, then they simply didn't complete their due diligence in protecting the people of San Bernardino.

But the San Bernardino shooting was one incident, and that incident exists on the backdrop of the entire landscape of California's instances of violence, crime, and protection in the face of guns. Overall, California's violent crime rate in 2014 was lower than that of Texas but higher than that of Georgia. But in 2011, California's murder by gun rate was higher than that of Texas and lower than that of Georgia, thus showing the complexity of describing the relation between gun access and crime.

In spite of the obtainability of guns, some gun control advocates hope for a harm reduction approach. Banning particularly damaging guns would mean both fewer deaths and less damaging injuries. Gun users who mean to do harm would be less effective, and

## CLOSING LOOPHOLES

Despite having waiting periods before someone can buy a gun and instituting background checks, there are loopholes in the legal system that can permit people to buy guns with little or no restrictions at all. Gun shows are often the place where these loopholes can be found. For instance, gun shows may have legal, certified dealers selling to other licensed retailers. A background check must be done on the retailer to make sure the he or she is buying legally. A Firearms Transaction Record must be filled out to keep a record of the transfer of firearms from one party to another. However, individuals attending the shows for private purposes are not subject to the same checks and regulations, and they are not

(*continued on the next page*)

*(continued from the previous page)* required to complete the Firearms Transaction Record. This loophole allows for undocumented transactions to private parties. Gun control advocates see gun shows as a way for criminals to get their hands on guns legally and without the same restrictions as buying a gun outside of a gun show. Many Second Amendment advocates feel that closing the gun show loophole with more legislation would mean interfering with Second Amendment rights.

Gun shows like this have less strict requirements for sales than stores that sell guns on their own premises.

users who care about protection would have just what they need for the intended purpose. Unfortunately, many advocates on both sides are not interested in a middle ground.

# MORE GUNS: PREVENTING VIOLENCE OR CAUSING IT?

When crimes that involve guns occur in the United States, the same question often surfaces: What could have been done to prevent it? Invariably, the idea of having an armed person on the scene to subdue the shooter in the case of a mass shooting gets discussed. Police often can't get to the scene soon enough, so people suggest that responsible, law-abiding citizens trained in firearms could, and should, intervene.

It has even been suggested that teachers carry guns or keep them available at schools to stop school shootings. Many teachers feel uncomfortable with this idea because it puts dangerous weapons in a safe school environment, and it would force teachers to take on a role in their classrooms that they may not be trained or emotionally equipped to deal with. For gun control advocates, the idea of introducing even more guns to deal with a gun violence problem is counterproductive.

When it comes to attacks on private places, like a person's home, adding guns to the equation can go either way. According to *Newsweek* magazine, "A study of 198 cases of unwanted entry into occupied single-family dwellings in Atlanta (not limited to night when the residents were sleeping) found that the invader was twice as likely to obtain the victim's gun than to have the victim use a firearm in self-defense." From there, violence can easily escalate to a fatal act of protection or

*A criminal illegally entering someone's home could be after anything—someone's property, money, or even someone's life.*

burglary. The potential for such encounters is clear from the fact that 36 percent of American adults either own their own firearm or live with someone who owns one. In fact, the overall rate of gun ownership in the United States remains fairly constant.

This statistic of how frequently a gun owner's weapon can be retrieved by a burglar is in stark contrast to chapter 3's assertion that guns protect people eighty times more than any other purpose. However, both of these may be true because the gun owners in their homes in Atlanta are a small sample of the American landscape of gun owners, and instances of burglary are a similarly limited lens through which to establish trends for crime. Or, it may be that the disproportionate reporting of crimes in different regions cause such great disparities in the data, meaning different places may have different needs. Advocates and opponents of gun control should acknowledge these differences and issues in data.

# 10 GREAT QUESTIONS TO ASK A LEGISLATOR ABOUT GUN CONTROL

1. Is it possible to have gun control laws that do not violate our Second Amendment rights?
2. What are your beliefs about the current gun control laws in this state?
3. What would you like to see changed about our state and local laws?
4. Why should a citizen vote for you and your position about guns and gun control?
5. What can I do to make changes in gun control laws in my state?
6. What kind of gun violence has our state seen in the past five years? What about the past ten years?
7. What is the consequence for someone found guilty of illegal firearms purchases in our state?
8. What is the consequence for someone found guilty of unlawful gun violence in our state?
9. Do you think any of our state's current gun control laws violate the Second Amendment? Why or why not?
10. Where can I learn more about gun control laws being proposed in our state?

CHAPTER FIVE

# WHAT CAN I DO ABOUT GUN VIOLENCE?

Americans would like to see less of the harm and crime that stems from the use of guns. Luckily, everyone can make an effort to make changes in the system. Depending on your position, that may mean wanting laws introduced or laws repealed, and appealing to a representative to act on your behalf. You may also benefit from acting on a grassroots level to increase awareness for various issues to do with guns. Here are some ways to achieve these goals.

## BE EDUCATED

One of the most important things people can do to promote a cause they are serious about is to become educated about it. First, learn about both sides of the issue. People interested in gun control can learn from those who feel strongly about the Second Amendment. Similarly, those interested in prioritizing Second Amendment protections afforded by the constitution should consider the point of view of gun control advocates so their own

# WHAT CAN I DO ABOUT GUN VIOLENCE? | 43

opinions are as informed as possible. Answering to the facts and statistics that the other side can present to the issue is likely to be more convincing than getting angry and failing to offer a persuasive response. And like all conversations, speaking with those who oppose your views requires respect.

Education about guns also includes knowledge about how to properly and safely use firearms. Even if you do not wish to use a gun, a person interested in gun control laws should be familiar with the various kinds of guns on the market and how they differ. Knowledge of guns, their capabilities, their popularity, and their uses can help make a person

Education about guns, including how to store and handle them, is a helpful way to reduce deaths from gun violence.

understand their appeal and why some might be more dangerous than helpful. Being aware of proper storage methods can help prevent accidents from happening, and research would reveal state, federal, and local laws that users should comply with.

If the issue of gun violence is centered on the fact that people choose to use guns for illicit purposes, then the reason for resorting to guns should be addressed. Other than changing laws and participating in a political capacity, knowing the signs of someone who is approaching a crisis can prevent a tragedy from occurring. Has someone made threats? Does this person express suicidal ideations? Is there an unusual fixation with violence or guns? Listening, and knowing what to listen for, can reveal a need for intervention for someone who is likely to commit a horrible act. This is a particularly interpersonal component that can make a positive difference in someone's personal life, but be sure to let in an adult (perhaps a parent or school administrator) to make decisions regarding reporting such incidents to the police or a mental health specialist.

Government institutions or nonprofit organizations can arrange for police or other trainers to talk to students about what to do and think about during a shooting, or how to spot signs of danger in a person's demeanor. They might teach how to seek shelter and where to go after an event to report a crime, or how to alert a person's loved ones of that person's safety.

# SURVIVE

One other important aspect of education is knowing what to do if you find yourself on the wrong side of a gun, as a potential victim. In the case of mass violence or gang violence, a large, public place like a school or theater or open street supplies an environment in which those present can run away if there is somewhere to escape to. Running is the best option so that you can remove yourself from the danger. Run in a zigzag pattern if the shooter is visible because those sideways movements would be difficult for a shooter to aim at. But do keep in mind that there might be other people running away, so be careful not to trip over them. Call 911 once clearly out of danger.

Hiding is also a good option, but only if running wouldn't bring those trying to escape to a clearly safe area. Being quiet is essential to not attracting the attention of a shooter, so don't call 911 until sufficiently barricaded in a hiding spot.

Finally, as a last resort, when trapped in a reachable area and being approached by the gunman, pose an attack (preferably a surprise), and fight the gunman as a group. Aim for the hands, eyes, neck, and nose to take control of the weapon and neutralize the threat.

Be sure to take into account everything you know about your surroundings, such as exits, hiding places, and potential weapons when deciding on a line of action.

If the violence is clearly targeted only at you (i.e., not an indiscriminate mass shooting or a gang shooting) and is in close quarters, like during a robbery on the street, it may be too late to take evasive action. It is best to let the robber (or culprit of a different type of crime) do what they want so that they feel less inclined to harm you—unless, of course, they have already expressed the intent to end your life. Close range shooters are much less likely to miss, but it may be that they are only interested in separating you from your wallet, jewelry, or some other item that is much more expendable than your life. Even in the case of such extreme violence as rape, not fighting an attacker who has a weapon is the best bet for at least surviving the encounter.

If the shooter is interested only in self-harm, it may be that the person can be talked down from the act. Something has been going on in that person's life, and gaining some understanding from a peer about one's struggles can make a big difference. It is unlikely that someone can reach a person who has put suicide into motion before it is too late, but knowing the signs of depression and looking out for expressions of self-loathing offers some substantial information to suggest the need of an intervention before those feelings go too far. And knowing measures such as CPR, how to stop bleeding, and other medical applications can save a life.

## SOCIAL AND POLITICAL ENGAGEMENT

A lobbyist is a paid professional who works for an organization and communicates and meets with lawmakers in government offices to discuss making changes in laws. In addition to changing the law, they work to shape public opinion.

Lobbying in the local, state, and national levels of government is an influential way to inform lawmakers about the positions of the lobbyist. Lobbyists may bring statistics about gun control or Second Amendment rights, and make presentations to try to shape the lawmaker's decisions. Some lobbyists even contribute money to political campaigns and try to increase their influence on the politicians and issues they wish to bring awareness to. The NRA is the most influential lobbyist group for promoting Second Amendment rights, while the biggest gun control lobby group is the Brady Campaign to Prevent Gun Violence. Although lobbying is a paid profession that adults do, underaged people can make a difference in supporting the activities of the lobbyists and reaching out to political candidates.

Starting a gun safety awareness club at school can also make a big difference. It will bring people together to talk about issues to do with guns, potentially creating an atmosphere in which there can be a meaningful debate that enriches both sides. Some activities might include arranging a presentation by police about the safe and proper storage of guns or showing films that explore the uses or dangers of guns. A presentation can help gun-owning parents of especially vulnerable young children, and it can promote gun safety.

It's important to get involved in the political process by learning about potential candidates and their views on gun control. Active young people can support the organizations and candidates that match their ideals,

James Brady (*pictured*) is the White House press secretary who was disabled during an assassination attempt on President Ronald Reagan in 1981.

and influence those who do vote and those who make laws even before they reach voting age. Speaking to Congress members or local assembly members, or even writing letters can make a huge difference.

Don't be discouraged, however, if you cannot influence lawmakers to take direct action. Working with an adult and getting involved in demonstrations that make your opinions known is part of other constitutional freedoms—freedom of speech and equal protection. Every person in America, from citizens to undocumented residents, has a right to voice non-threatening opinions and protest the government.

Protesting is one of the most visible and vocal ways for people to voice their opinions about an issue.

## SEEKING HELP

After a tragic event, psychological manifestations of trauma, like post-traumatic stress disorder, can appear. Symptoms such as nightmares, loss of sleep, fear and anxiety, or loss of appetite can plague people who were close to the event. The reality of the shooting or violent event makes them think that they could have easily been a victim or placed in a more dangerous situation, and the feeling of reliving the event can cause psychological

### GABBY GIFFORDS

One of the most vocal gun-control advocates is United States politician Gabby Giffords, who was also a victim of gun violence in 2011. As a member of Arizona's eighth district, the congresswoman was taking part in a community event with the public that involved meeting local constituents. It was there that gunman Jared Lee Loughner fired into the crowd, killing six people and injuring nineteen others. Giffords was shot through the skull and spent years recovering from the brain injury, including learning to speak again. Today, she is an advocate for gun control along with her husband, astronaut Mark Kelly. They cofounded an organization called Americans for Responsible Solutions. They feel that electing officials who can vote for gun control measures will help improve the problem of gun violence in America.

harm. Even when people do not know those who were involved in the shootings, the idea that such a violent event took place at their school or among their peers is difficult for many people to handle.

These feelings are why social workers and psychologists are usually made available to students who wish to talk about what happened in their school or community. Healing from gun violence is a long process, and it's one that should definitely include professional help.

Support groups for people involved in gun violence can also help people deal with the aftereffects. Young people can work with a school psychologist, social

These people are seeking psychological help in group therapy. They are participating in an important part of the healing process.

worker, or guidance counselor to cope with the pain of physical trauma or traumatic memories, or they can seek out these professionals in their schools to help them find different mental health professionals. Group therapy is also available at a cheaper cost than one-on-one sessions with a mental health professional.

## CONCLUSION

There is one ultimate change that can settle the gun debate once and for all: a strong consensus. A concensus would allow for a measure that abolishes guns, removes all restrictions from accessing and using them, or something in between. Or, it could allow free access to guns and other weapons. Such a decision is far on the horizon, so being prepared for the current climate is the best that the present can offer in the realm of political life. For now, knowing what to do if gun violence should reach your doorstep is the greatest protection for the worst of social situations.

But that means now is the time to deal with the present outcomes. Standing up to be heard is one of the most important things that a person can do, and enthusiasm and strong arguments can influence adults to take action. Whether favoring a different approach to a locality's gun regulations, figuring how to reach out to distressed individuals, or figuring out how to cope with something that is in the past, make your needs clear to those around you. Encourage others to speak out with you when you try to make them recognize both your needs and the reasons you want to see change. Let the world know that the issues and events surrounding gun activity affect you and that you know you deserve better. It's difficult work, but reaching the ideal outcome isn't guaranteed without a mobilized and energized public working toward resolving the issue.

# GLOSSARY

**advocate** A person who supports a particular cause or policy; the act of supporting a cause or policy.
**assault weapon** Term used to describe some semi-automatic firearms used for commercial use.
**automatic weapon** A firearm that fires rounds continuously when the trigger is held down.
**background check** The process of looking up a person's name in databases for criminal records or other information about a person.
**concealed weapon** A weapon that is hidden from sight.
**First Amendment** Amendment to US Constitution that provides to citizens the freedoms of religion, speech, and press.
**gun license** A permit given to a person to allow the purchase or ownership of a firearm.
**gun permit** An official document granting permission for someone to own or purchase a firearm.
**homicide** Intentionally and unlawfully killing someone.
**legislation** A law or a group of laws.
**lobbyist** A paid professional from an organization that attempts to persuade legislation.
**loophole** An unclear or unsatisfactory set of rules.
**mass shooting** A shooting of four or more people in a public place.
**militia** A military force populated by civilians who have united.
**National Rifle Association (NRA)** Organization that supports the protection of gun rights.

**post-traumatic stress disorder** A condition of continuing mental or emotional stress resulting from a violent, dangerous, or stressful situation.

**repeal** To reverse or end the effectiveness of a law.

**Second Amendment** Amendment to US Constitution that provides citizens with the right to keep and bear arms.

**semiautomatic weapon** A firearm that loads automatically but requires some manual operation.

**Stand Your Ground laws** Self-defense laws that enable a person to defend themselves to prevent death or great bodily harm.

## Americans for Responsible Solutions
PO Box 15642
Washington, DC 20003
(571) 295-7807
Website: http://americansforresponsiblesolutions.org
Americans for Responsible Solutions is a nonprofit organization that supports gun control while also supporting and protecting the right to responsible gun ownership.

## The Brady Campaign to Prevent Gun Violence
840 First Street NE
Suite 400
Washington, DC 20002
(202) 370-8100
Website: http://www.bradycampaign.org
The Brady Campaign to Prevent Gun Violence is a lobby group promoting gun control regulations in the United States.

## National Rifle Association
11250 Waples Mill Road
Fairfax, VA 22030
(800) 672-3888
Website: https://explore.nra.org
The National Rifle Association is a lobbying group dedicated to protecting Second Amendment rights in the United States. It offers training in safe gun usage.

**Royal Canadian Mounted Police**
National Headquarters Building
73 Leikin Drive
Ottawa, ON K1A 0R2
Canada
(613) 993-7267
Website: http://www.rcmp-grc.gc.ca
The Royal Canadian Mounted Police is the organization responsible for providing and renewing firearm licenses in Canada, and for providing information about firearms laws in Canada.

**Violence Policy Center**
1730 Rhode Island Avenue NW
Suite 1014
Washington, DC 20036
(202) 822-8200
Website: http://www.vpc.org
Violence Policy Center is an organization dedicated to lobbying legislators and informing the public about the effects of gun violence.

# WEBSITES

Because of the changing nature of internet links, Rosen Publishing has developed an online list of websites related to the subject of this book. This site is updated regularly. Please use this link to access the list:

http://www.rosenlinks.com/NTKL/guns

Bjorklund, Ruth. *Gun Control* (Debating the Issues). New York, NY: Cavendish Square Publishing, 2014.
Cullen, David. *Columbine.* New York, NY: Twelve Publishers, 2010.
Hand, Carol. *Gun Control and the Second Amendment.* Edina, MN: Essential Press, 2016.
Merino, Noel. *Gun Control* (Introducing Issues with Opposing Viewpoints). Farmington Hills, MI: Greenhaven Press, 2012.
Nakaya, Andrea C. *Mass Shootings.* San Diego, CA: Referencepoint Press, 2015.
Netzley, Patricia. *Can Gun Control Reduce Violence?* San Diego, CA: Referencepoint Press, 2013.
Scherer, Lauri. *Gun Violence* (Issues that Concern You). Farmington Hills, MI: Greenhaven Press, 2012.
Schildkraut, Jacklyn. *Mass Shootings: Media, Myths, and Realities.* Santa Barbara, CA: Praeger, 2016.
Torres, John Albert. *The People Behind School Shootings and Public Massacres.* Berkeley Heights, NJ: Enslow Publishing, 2016.
Watkins, Christine. *Guns and Crime.* Farmington Hills, MI: Greenhaven Press, 2012.
Wolny, Philip. *Gun Rights: Interpreting the Constitution.* New York, NY: Rosen Classroom, 2014.

Bearing Arms. "Harvard: Gun Control Doesn't Work." August 25, 2013. http://bearingarms.com/ba-staff/2013/08/25/harvard-gun-control-doesnt-work/.

Brady Campaign to Prevent Gun Violence. "Key Gun Violence Statistics." Retrieved November 12, 2016. http://www.bradycampaign.org/key-gun-violence-statistics.

Donohue, John. "Gun Control: What the US Can Learn from Other Advanced Countries." *Newsweek*, October 3, 2015. http://www.newsweek.com/gun-control-what-we-can-learn-other-advanced-countries-379105.

Ferriss, Susan. "NRA Pushed 'Stand Your Ground' Laws Across the Nation." Juvenile Justice Information Exchange, March 31, 2012. http://jjie.org/nra-pushed-stand-your-ground-laws-across-nation/80738/.

Fifield, Anna. "In Japan, Even the Gun Enthusiasts Welcome Restrictions on Firearms." June 29, 2015. https://www.washingtonpost.com/world/in-japan-even-the-gun-enthusiasts-are-in-favor-of-gun-control/2015/06/27/283cfaea-19a6-11e5-bed8-1093ee58dad0_story.html.

FindLaw. "States That Have Stand Your Ground Laws." Retrieved November 12, 2016. http://criminal.findlaw.com/criminal-law-basics/states-that-have-stand-your-ground-laws.html.

Gun Owners of America. "Fact Sheet: Guns Save Lives." Retrieved November 12, 2016. https://www.gunowners.org/sk0802htm.htm.

Hallowell, Billy. "The History and Evolution of Guns as Told Through Pictures." Blaze, March 12, 2013. http://www.theblaze.com/stories/2013/03/12/the-history-and-evolution-of-guns-as-told-through-pictures/.

History. "Gatling Gun." Retrieved January 3, 2017. http://www.history.com/topics/gatling-gun.

Israel, Steve. "Guns: Thousands of Americans Die, and Yet We Do Nothing." CNN, December 3, 2015. http://www.cnn.com/2015/10/04/opinions/steve-israel-thousands-die-america-doesnt-act/index.html.

Kessler, Glenn. "Was the 'Stand Your Ground' Law the 'Cause' of Trayvon Martin's Death?" *Washington Post*, October 29, 2014. https://www.washingtonpost.com/news/fact-checker/wp/2014/10/29/was-the-stand-your-ground-law-the-cause-of-trayvon-martins-death/.

Kurtzleben, Danielle. "Here's Where Gun Laws Stand in Your State." NPR, June 14, 2016. http://www.npr.org/2015/12/09/458829225/heres-where-gun-laws-stand-in-your-state.

Law Center to Prevent Gun Violence. "Statistics on Gun Deaths & Injuries." Retrieved January 3, 2017. http://smartgunlaws.org/gun-deaths-and-injuries-statistics/.

Laws. "How to Get a Gun License." Retrieved November 12, 2016. http://gun.laws.com/gun-license.

Masters, Jonathan. "How Do U.S. Gun Laws Compare to Other Countries?" *PBS NewsHour,* June 13, 2016. http://www.pbs.org/newshour/rundown/how-do-u-s-gun-laws-compare-to-other-countries/.

Masters, Kate. "New CDC Report Shows America's Gun Suicide Problem Getting Worse." The Trace, April 26, 2016. https://www.thetrace.org/2016/04/cdc-study-gun-suicides-getting-worse/.

McIntire, Mike. "Weapons in San Bernardino Shootings Were Legally Obtained." *New York Times*, December 3, 2015. http://www.nytimes.com/2015/12/04/us/weapons-in-san-bernardino-shootings-were-legally-obtained.html.

National Institute of Justice. "Gun Violence." April 4, 2013. https://www.nij.gov/topics/crime/gun-violence/Pages/welcome.aspx.

*PBS NewsHour*. "It's the Weapon of Choice for U.S. Mass Murders: The AR-15." June 14, 2016. http://www.pbs.org/newshour/bb/its-the-weapon-of-choice-for-u-s-mass-murderers-the-ar-15/.

UC Davis Health System. "UC Davis Report Exposes Loopholes in Gun-control Laws." Retrieved-November 12, 2016. http://www.ucdmc.ucdavis.edu/welcome/features/20090923_gun_study/.

## A

accidental shootings, 18, 21, 27
Americans for Responsible Solutions, 50
AR-15, 12–13, 14
automatic weapons, 11, 12, 19, 30, 36

## B

Brady Handgun Violence Prevention Act of 1993, 14

## C

Canada, gun control laws in, 30–32
Civil War, 11
Columbine High School shooting, 21, 23
concealed weapons, 15

## F

Farook, Syed, 36
flintlock pocket pistol, 10–11

## G

gangs, 5, 18, 19–20
Gatling gun, 11
Giffords, Gabby, 50

Gun Control Act of 1968, 14
gun safety awareness club, starting, 47
gun shows, 37–38
gun violence statistics, 4, 20–21, 27, 29, 39–40

## H

Harris, Eric, 23

## I

Israel, gun control laws in, 32

## J

Japan, gun control laws in, 31–32, 33

## K

Klebold, Dylan, 23

## L

Lanza, Adam, 24

## M

Malik, Tashfeen, 36
Martin, Trayvon, 17
mass shooting statistics, 5, 21–23

Mateen, Omar, 24–25
militia, explanation of, 8
muskets, 10, 11

# N

National Rifle Association, 15

# O

Obama, Barack, 23

# P

Pulse nightclub shooting, 21, 24–25

# R

Russia, gun control laws in, 14–15
Ryan, Michael Robert, 32

# S

San Bernardino, CA, shooting, 36
Sandy Hook Elementary School shooting, 21, 24
Scott, Walter, 22
Second Amendment, 8, 9, 14, 15, 18, 38, 42
semiautomatic weapons, 12, 14, 24, 30, 32, 36
Slager, Michael, 22
Stand Your Ground laws, 16–17

state laws, 15, 16–17, 34–36
suicide, 5–6, 18, 21, 27

# U

United Kingdom, gun control laws in, 32–33

# Z

Zimmerman, George, 17

## ABOUT THE AUTHOR

Adam Furgang attended the High School of Art and Design and the University of the Arts. He has worked as a graphic designer, web designer, fine artist, freelance photographer, and writer. He has written extensively for the middle school market, including nonfiction titles and an upper middle grade novel, *Braxton Woods Mystique*. He also runs a creative blog, wizardsneverwearamor.com, which concentrates on topics such as gaming, art, films, and pop culture. He lives in upstate New York with his wife and two sons.

## PHOTO CREDITS

Cover © iStockphoto.com/BlakeDavidTaylor; back cover photo by Marianna Armata/Moment/Getty Images; p. 5 Nicholas Kamm/AFP/Getty Images; pp. 7, 18, 27, 34, 42 (background) Bezikus/Shutterstock.com; p. 9 © North Wind Picture Archives; p. 10 Military Images/Alamy Stock Photo; p. 13 Hindustan Times/Getty Images; p. 16 Anadolu Agency/Getty Images; p. 19 Boston Globe/Getty Images; p. 22 Richard Ellis/Getty Images; p. 25 ©AP Images; p. 28 GaryAlvis/E+/Getty Images; p. 30 Anton Kudelin/Shutterstock.com; p. 31 Ulrich Niehoff/ImageBroker/Getty Images; p. 35 Getty Images; p. 38 The Washington Post/Getty Images; p. 40 Photographee.eu/Shutterstock.com; p. 43 Monkey Business Images/Getty Images; p. 48 Ron Galella, Ltd./Getty Images; p. 49 © iStockphoto.com/EyeJoy; p. 51 © iStockphoto.com/Asiseeit.

Design: Michael Moy; Layout Design: Tahara Anderson; Editor: Bernadette Davis; Photo Researcher: Sherri Jackson

MAY - - 2018